Based on
The Railway Series
by the
Rev. W. Awdry

Illustrations by
**Robin Davies and
Jerry Smith**

EGMONT

Gordon was surprised to see the broken-down engine was **Spencer**!

"I've no water," Spencer snapped. "My tank must be leaking!"

Gordon smiled. "We must hurry. Everyone is waiting for the Duke and Duchess."

Soon Gordon was coupled up to Spencer and they **steamed** away.

Minutes later, they pulled into Maron Station — just in time for the party!

"Well done, Gordon," said The Fat Controller. "You are a **Really Useful Engine**!"

Gordon blew his whistle loudly. "**Poooop!** Thank you, Sir."

The next day it was Spencer who was feeling happy. His Driver told him that he was an even faster engine than Gordon.

"I'm the **fastest** and **finest** engine on Sodor!" Spencer boasted.

The Fat Controller's engines were very cross.

Spencer was taking the Duke and Duchess to their summer house. The Fat Controller needed another engine to carry their furniture.

All the engines wanted the chance to **race** Spencer, but The Fat Controller chose old Edward.

"Edward is so slow. He'll lose the race and make our Railway look silly!" groaned James.

Thomas and Percy were cross with James. Edward was their friend.

"Don't listen to James," they told Edward. "You can beat that **BIG silver show-off!**"

Edward set off slowly and steadily, but Spencer steamed quickly past him. With a **whoosh**, Spencer was gone!

Edward's train was heavy. His **axles ached** and his **wheels wobbled**.

But then he saw Donald and Douglas cheering him on. "You can beat Spencer!" they called.

This made Edward feel much better. He **huffed** and **puffed** to the top of the next hill. Then he raced down the other side!

Just ahead was Spencer. While the Duke and Duchess were taking photos, Spencer was having a rest. He had fallen **fast asleep!**

Spencer didn't hear Edward puff past him. He was too busy dreaming about winning!

When he opened his eyes, he couldn't believe it — Edward was in the lead.

"Nearly there, nearly there," gasped Edward.

Spencer steamed off as **fast** as his wheels would carry him, but he was too late.

Edward pulled to a stop in front of the summer house. "I've won!" he smiled.

Edward's **axles** didn't **ache** anymore and his **wheels** weren't **wobbling**. He felt like the pride of Sodor Railway! And Spencer felt very silly.

More about Spencer

- funnel
- nameplate
- whistle
- cab
- tender
- cylinders
- buffer
- coupling hook

Spencer's challenge to you

Look back through the pages of this book and see if you can spot:

luggage

birds

bunting

mountain

flowers

ADVERTISEMENT

THE THOMAS ENGINE ADVENTURES

From Thomas to Harold the Helicopter, there is an Engine Adventure to thrill every Thomas fan.

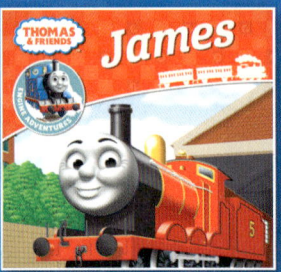
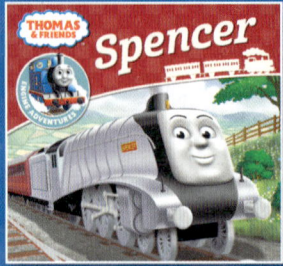